S0-CAJ-507

Incognito Mosquito
Makes History

"I laughed so hard I almost lost my head!"
—*Marie Antoinette*

"A masterpiece!" —*Tickelangelo*

"A symphony in puns!"

ig van Beetlethoven

Incognito Mosquito Makes History

by E. A. Hass
illustrated by Don Madden

RANDOM HOUSE 🏠 NEW YORK

To Mark L. Levine
with fondest litigations

Text copyright © 1987 by E.A. Hass.
Illustrations copyright © 1987 by Random House, Inc.
All rights reserved under International and Pan-American Copyright
Conventions. Published in the United States by Random House, Inc., New
York, and simultaneously in Canada by Random House of Canada Limited,
Toronto.

Library of Congress Cataloging in Publication Data:
Hass, E.A.
  Incognito Mosquito makes history.
  SUMMARY: The famous insective, Incognito Mosquito, travels back in time
to solve five mysteries involving such notables as Christopher Columbug,
Benetick Arnold, Buffalo Bill Cootie, Tutankhamant, and Robin Hoodlum.
  [1. Mosquitoes—Fiction. 2. Insects—Fiction. 3. Mystery and detective
stories] I. Madden, Don, ill. II. Title.
PZ7.H2768Imk 1987 [Fic] 86-20417
ISBN: 0-394-87055-7 (pbk); 0-394-97055-1 (lib. bdg.)

Manufactured in the United States of America
1 2 3 4 5 6 7 8 9 0

Contents

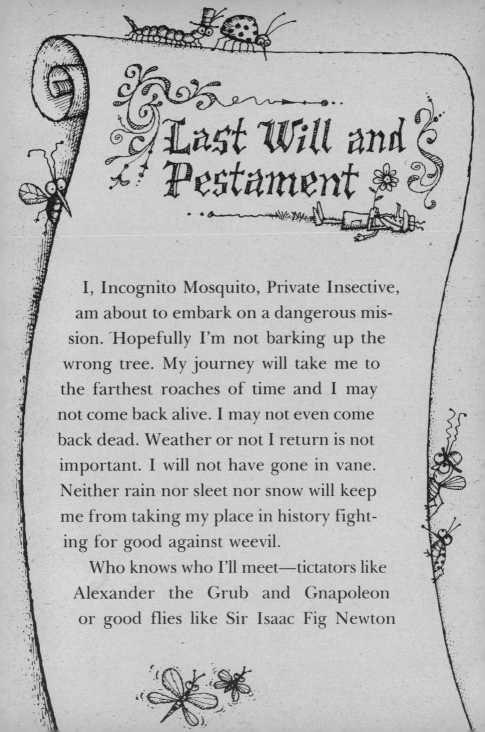

Last Will and Pestament

I, Incognito Mosquito, Private Insective, am about to embark on a dangerous mission. Hopefully I'm not barking up the wrong tree. My journey will take me to the farthest roaches of time and I may not come back alive. I may not even come back dead. Weather or not I return is not important. I will not have gone in vane. Neither rain nor sleet nor snow will keep me from taking my place in history fighting for good against weevil.

Who knows who I'll meet—tictators like Alexander the Grub and Gnapoleon or good flies like Sir Isaac Fig Newton and Alexander Graham Cracker, world-famous cookie discoverers. Whoever, I swear to keep buzzy solving mysteries and spreading sweetness and lice throughout the ages.

Should I not return, I bequeath all my worldly belongings to the American No-see-um of Natural Mystery. A small plaque to that effect wouldn't hurt either.

Signed : *Incognito Mosquito*
Witlessed : *Incognito Mosquito*

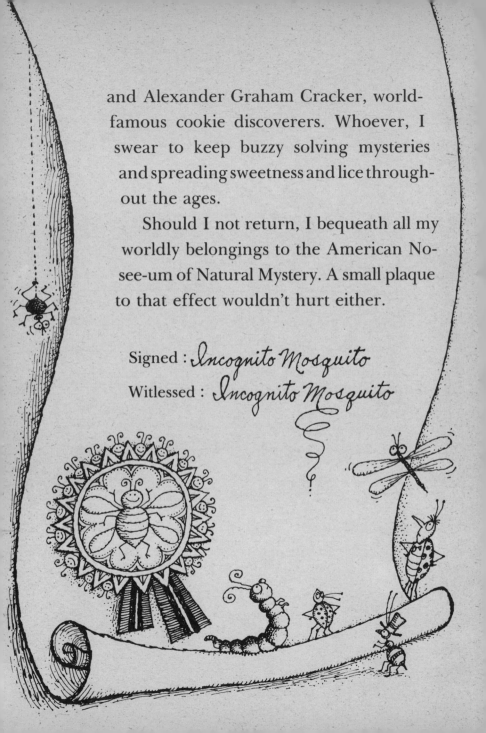

Allow me to introduce my-self: T.C. Fly. But the other kids just call me Encentepedia Bug. I guess it's because I'm such a bookworm. And I love a good mystery. That's why I was so thrilled—at least at first—when I stumbled onto the hive of Incognito Mosquito, who had stumbled onto more mysteries than I could count.

Let me start from the beginning. I first met Incognito Mosquito, Private Insec-tive, a few days ago. Was it only that long ago? I tend to lose track of time recently. When I've told you my story, I suspect you will too. You see, time is what this story is all about. . . .

I was working my way through my summer vacation by selling subscriptions to *Flyantific American* when I randomly chose to ring the buzzer of this particular apartment. I had no idea of its occupant, since the little slot where the name usually is said "Wouldn't you like to know!" I had a hunch that this was no ordinary apartment when I got a recorded message asking for my name, address, telephone

number, anti-social insecurity number, place of hatching, and branch of family tree. But I guess I passed the test, because I soon heard footsteps and someone—or something—fiddling with the locks. There were lots of locks.

Looking down, I noticed that a strange-looking multicolored smoke was seeping under the door, and a purplish glop was gradually approaching my shoes. Boy! It looked like I'd caught a live one this time.

Just then the door opened slowly with a terrifying creak. I pictured all kinds of horrible creatures inside—robots, ghouls, monsters, mad scientists. . . . Imagine my disappointment when this lone mosquito appeared. He invited me into his cluttered apartment and I introduced myself. "Hello there, sir," I said, starting off the memorized sales pitch I'd been given. "You look like an intelligent bug, eager to know what's

happening in the world around, above, and
underneath you . . ." But it was almost im-
possible to continue. For one thing, all these
wild smells were coming from the next
room, not to mention the multicolored
smoke and purplish goop. Also, I couldn't
keep a straight face looking at the mosquito. He was wearing a ridiculous out-of-
this-world helmet. Until he took it off, I
thought it was his head!

The mosquito noticed my interest and
introduced himself by saying, "Incognito
Mosquito's my name, time-travel private
insecting's my game."

6

"Wow!" I said. I took a few deep breaths and cleared my throat and asked Mr. Mosquito what was in the next room. Obligingly, he gave me a tour of his lab. Wow! It was amazing!

The lab was a mess of test tubes, brightly colored solutions bubbling all over the place, and odds and ends of all kinds of equipment thrown around the room. The only thing missing was the kitchen ... wait—there was the sink, too. The purplish stuff that had begun climbing up my pants was coming from a flask sitting on a Bunsen burner. The Mosquito reached over and turned it off absentmindedly, explaining, "It's my new recipe for travel fuel. Guess I put too much yeast in it. Rising too fast."

The Mosquito told me he had taken up time travel as a sort of hobby. As he explained it, "I found stump collecting too treedious. And in between losing clients to nervous breakdowns, I made a break-through!"

I wasn't sure what breakthrough he was talking about, and to tell you the truth, I was afraid to ask as I looked around his totally weird lab. But what caught my eye was IT. It was huge, shiny, and made up of almost anything—and everything—you could think of. Dozens of what I assumed were spare parts lay all over the floor and half in and half out of the machine.

"That is my time machine," Mr. Mosquito said proudly. "I call it the *Anterprise*. It's five-million-year mission is to explore new worms and new civilizations, to boldly go where no bug has gone before. Although I must say, that sounds like something I've heard before. James Flea Kirk, perhaps?

"Anyway, the whole machine is jet-powered," Incognito continued. "I got the idea when I went to Radio City Music Hall and saw the Rockettes. And it's so easy to operate! You see, you just push this red button here—or is it that blue switch there?

"Well, anyway, you just turn that dial clockwise to select the date in time you want to travel to and you turn this dial counterclockwise to find the place you want to go to . . . or was that clockwise for the place and counterclockwise for the . . . ? Say, maybe that's why I've been having trouble with the machine lately. I just washed it, and I can't do a thing with it!"

"Gee, Mr. Mosquito," I said, "I'm pretty good with these mechanical-type things. If you'd let me—"

"No, no thanks," the Mosquito said, patting me on the head. (Why do they always pat you on the head?) "This isn't child's play. Now, let's see. You put the socket in the sprocket . . . or do you jammer with the hammer . . . ?"

The Mosquito's confusion about the inner workings of rockets—not to mention the inner workings of his own brain—was starting to become clear to me. In fact, this bug was giving me atomic ache.

"Anyway," the Mosquito went on, "I built my *Anterprise* out of a variety of spare parts. I really started from scratch and I've been itching to tell someone about it."

Naturally I listened attentively. I didn't

want the Mosquito to realize that I'd begun to realize that the biggest mystery here was how he managed to solve mysteries in the first place. I sure didn't want to make him mad. After all, a mad scientist can spell big trouble. That's B-I-G T-R-O-U-B-L-E.

"You really have to be inventive to build a time machine," the Insective explained. "For example, this dry cell started out as evidence in one of my cases. Assault and battery, I think. The charges were dropped though. Not enough positive evidence. These wheels came from an old foreign sports car of mine. When I need something to stop the electric current from leaking, I use these old spark plugs. And I hooked up an old air conditioner to a pair of suspenders just the other day—does just dandy as a fan belt."

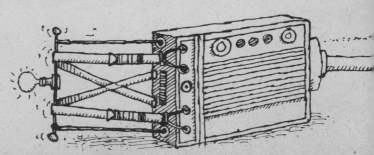

I stared in amazement. It was difficult
to believe that the pile of junk standing
before me could ever have transported the

bug through time. He had to be kidding. But I figured I'd humor him. A little good humor never hurt anyone. Sometimes it even gets you ice cream.

"How do you decide where to go in time?" I asked. "I mean, how do you know where there's a mystery that needs solving?"

"That's easy to answer. You see, all of life's a mystery to me, so I can find one anywhere. Like, the other day I was reading this book," the Mosquito said, pointing to a large volume on his desk. "*Moby Tick* by Vermin Melville. I found myself longing for the high seas. Or was it shorting for the low seas? No matter. I decided to give it a quick look-see and discover what antique-arium life was all about. So I just set the dial on the *Anterprise* for the age of the great sea explorers and bugged out for parts unknown . . ."

1
The Case of the Copped Compass

"Hey, flyzanno!" were the first words I heard when I woke up. And what a rude awakening it was. The bump I got from hitting the crow's-nest had knocked me even more unconscious than usual. Now here I was, all caught up in the ship's rigging. "Oh, what a tangled web we weave . . ." I thought, struggling to free myself.

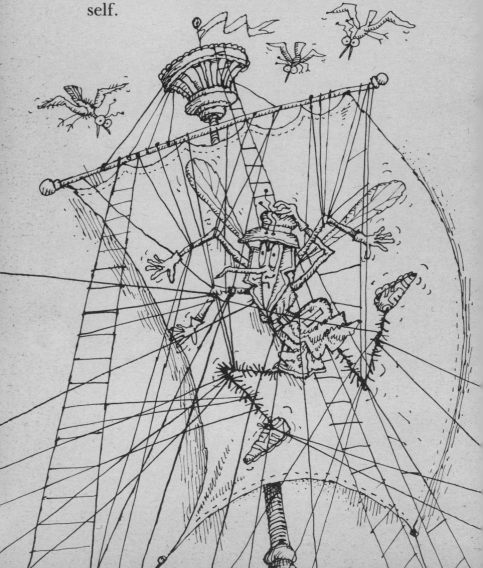

The moment I was cut down, I was brought before the captain of the fleet, one Christopher Columbug. THE Christopher Columbug! The same one you read about in history and geography books. The one who was financed by Queen Itchabella and King Ferdinant to sail west across the Atlantic and who quite by accident discovered the New Worm. Yes, I, Incognito Mosquito, had dropped in on the famed explorer during his quest for a shorter route to the East Indies. Or was it the West Outies?

Unfortunately, I hadn't brought my sea legs and I soon got very fleasick. Even more unfortunately the crew insisted on feeding me Italian delicacies "just lika Momma used to make." I didn't have the heart to tell them I was hatched. They kept giving me wormacelli, but it only made me riggletoni. We had to clean up the mess with a spongelli.

On the whole, though, I did swimmingly and time pasta quite quickly. I spent many hours watching Captain Columbug's navigational methods. It was amazing to see him calculate our position according to the heavenly bodies in the sky. After all, he had only the sun in the mooring and the moon for flight. Plus the few stars that captains used to navigate by—mainly the Big and Little Skipper.

Before long we hit land, a small island just off the mainland. It was still winter, but this place was no Ice Cuba. We found the weather balmy. Not to mention palmy.

When I saw the crowd of Indians who came out to meet us, I had some reservations. The place looked a bit hostile for a hostel. But I needn't have worried. The Indians were as hospitable as could be. It wasn't long before we were all sitting around the old wigworm, dressed in ceremonial bugskins. They even offered me a headdress. I almost took it. It would have been a real feather in my cap. I was tickled at the offer. But, at the risk of skirting the issue, I felt funny about the dress part.

It turned out that we had arrived on the island just after the Indians. One tribe had come all the way from what would later be known as Cleveland. Another group had just paddled in from what was to be called Atlanta. Seems the Cleveland Indians and the Atlanta Braves met there every spring to practice some simple type of game— basicball. The game was just in its infancy and their stadium was built out of odds and ends. Still, the Indians were very proud of Tidbits Field.

Spring training was just beginning, and the two teams were about to play their first game. I was asked to throw the first ball! "May the pest team win," I yelled out as I let the ball fly.

The game was very exciting. Time after

time the basics were loaded. All the big play-ers were there—Fly Cobb, Joe Dimaggoto, Willie Maysfly. Unfortunately, one of the favorites, Johnny, was benched. Seems he was sent to the boll pen because he'd played rookie once too often.

TIDBITS FIELD

All too soon we were into the seventh-inning stretch. The Polynesian cheer-leeches, specially imported from Hawaii, began practicing their new hula whoops. Columbug's Italian crew was busy promising the players their first taste of Righetti Spaghetti after the game.

Christopher Columbug and I were seated up in the stands with the Indian chief, Geroniroach. The explorer was telling the chief how excited Ferdinant and Itchabella would be about his discovery of the New Worm and that they would send over many visitors.

"How," the chief commented.

"Why, by boat, of course," Columbug replied. "Within a few years, Geroniroach, this could become the new Club Med! We'll have Mediterranean Fruit Flies swarming all over the place. This'll be the new island hide-away!"

Suddenly Geroniroach stood up and called a powwow in his wigworm. Dozens of Indians left the stands. They listened silently to Geroniroach's instructions. And then they scattered in all different directions. Columbug and I couldn't figure out what was going on! Until we returned to the ships after the game and found Columbug's compass missing.

Apparently some Indians sneaked aboard while we were at the game and took the compass. We knew the Indians were the culprits because they left fake clues just to confuse us. I found a pair of mock-assins.

This was serious. Without his compass, Christopher Columbug could never find his way home. He was stuck on the island—and so were we!

A thorough search of the area by the crew turned up nothing. I knew it was all up to me. I questioned several of the Indians. I even tried to threaten them. "You'd better play ball with me or else . . ." But the Indians really threw me a curve. They wouldn't say a word. I tried to squeeze the info out of a squaw named Fliawatha. But she refused to be squawshed.

I spoke with a young Indian named Tommy Hawk, who turned out to be the tribe hatchet man. He was no stool pigeon either. I tried to take him under my wing, but when I asked if he knew who'd done the robbin' he just shook his head and ran off raven'. In spite of my pleas not to be shut out, that interview was a real short stop.

I decided to try and beat the Indians at their own game—tracking. I would follow all the fresh footprints that led away from the water's edge. One set had to take me to

Columbug's compass. If only the Indians had not been such tricky trackmakers! There were hundreds of trails to follow. After a while, I wasn't sure whether I was coming or going. I rarely am.

Several hours later I followed a group of tracks that led to a pool of quicksand. Needless to say, I stopped short. Apparently the Indians had too. There were several sets of prints going up to the quicksand and then turning away. All except for one trail, which led up to the pool of quicksand and then . . . ended. I'd heard stories about bugs who were so desperate for a beach that they used the pool as a last resort.

Then I took a second look at that last set of prints. There was something different about them.

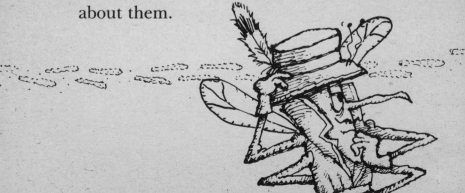

All of a sudden I knew I wasn't going to strike out after all. In fact, I was about to make the most amazing home run ever recorded. I was about to send Christopher Columbug and his ships back across the Atlantic Ocean!

WHAT DID INCOGNITO MOSQUITO REALIZE ABOUT THE FOOTPRINTS?

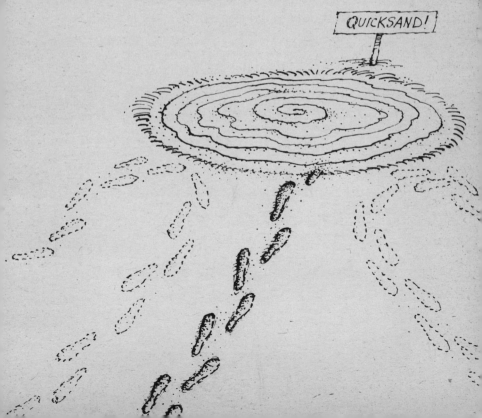

On closer examination, Incognito saw that the footprints in the trail that ended at the pool of quicksand were deeper than the other prints he'd seen. About twice as deep, in fact.

Incognito realized that a skillful Indian must have wanted it to look like he had jumped into the quicksand. Our hero concluded that this Indian had walked to the pool, and then walked away backward in his own tracks. That explained why one set of tracks was twice as deep as the others. Incognito simply followed those tracks, which led directly back to the tent of the Indian with the compass, one Pocahornet.

Naturally, Pocahornet was stinging mad when asked to surrender Columbug's property. She was almost ready to go to pieces. But after smoking the piece pipe, she put herself back together and vowed never to

try such a spec-track-ular heist again.

Geroniroach explained that he'd asked Pocahornet to hide the compass. He was afraid that the tiny island would be overrun by tourists if Columbug ever brought word of it back to Spain. Geroniroach was very impressed that Incognito was able to finger Pocahornet, hand over the compass, and nail the case shut.

To show his gratitude, Christopher Columbug renamed one of his ships. From that day forward, the three were known as the *Niña*, the *Pinta*, and the *Santa Mosquito*.

"**I** came pretty close to being all washed up in that case," the Mosquito said lightly. "Was almost beached. But as it turned out, I sailed right through it. The whole thing was a breeze. And we all had a merritime."

I had to admit, as questionable as his ability to travel through time was, Incognito Mosquito was one good storyteller. So just for kicks, I decided to play along with the bug as he tinkered with his broken machine.

Unfortunately, a kick was just what I got. Accidentally, the Mosquito leaned over

30

the machine's engine a bit too far and fell in, catching me in the antennae on the way down. Fortunately, it was only a nick, and in the nick of time I was able to catch one of his legs, keeping him from being discombobulated by the carburetor.

"Phew," he said, wiping his brow. "That was a close one!"

Calmly I asked, "What I don't understand, Mr. Mosquito, is how can you be sure that you're helping history, rather than hurting it? I mean, is it really fair to pop into another time zone and just fall into things the way you do?"

The Mosquito replied overheatedly, "Hurt history? How could I hurt it? After all, I know how the story's supposed to end, don't I?

"And you talk of fair. I'll tell you about fair. Do you think it's fair when an undercover spy—not even a bedbug, mind you—tries to smuggle top-secret information? Well, here, let me tell you all about it . . ."

2

The Case of the Traitorous Tick

It was dusk when I found myself floating in the middle of a harbor. I guess I should have known something was fishy when I pulled a herring out of my hat. But I didn't have much time to think about

33

it, because dozens of fleas were dumping huge chests of tea off the boats and onto my head. Everyone was hissing "No tixation without representation!" Louder and louder. Things were really coming to a boil.

I was about to ask for some sugar to go with the tea when one of the fleas gave it to me. Two lumps. Squarely on the head. With a chest. It was several minutes before I was able to stir. I was ready to bag it and

leaf the scene. "What a revolting development this is," I thought to myself.

When suddenly my eyes grew as wide as saucers. It hit me. Not the flea. An idea. I knew where I was. I had landed right in the middle of a revolt. This was the Evolutionary War! The American colonests were fighting the British Yellow Jackets for their independence. Why, this was the Boston Flea Party!

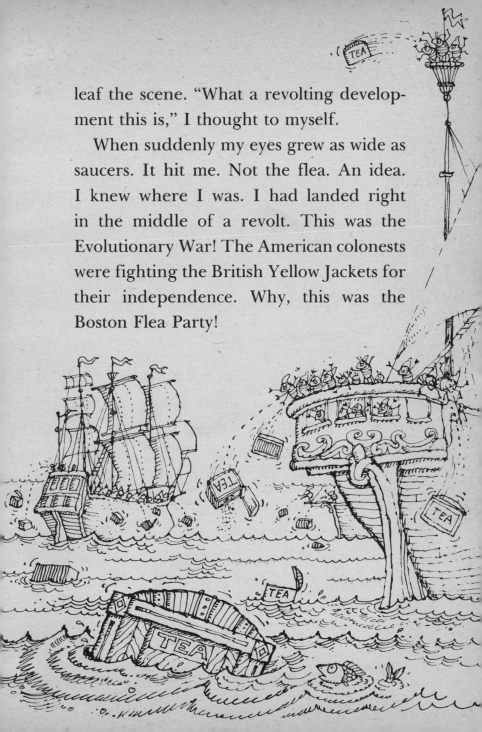

I climbed out of the water and was fortunately identified as a patriot by my three-cornered hat. Little did the fleas know I had only selected it to cover my pointed head! I'd just stopped to offer a tissue to the town crier when I heard "Psst, psst! C'mere." I looked around to see who was talking. All I could see was a ball of dirt. I gave it a nudge, but the smudge wouldn't budge.

"Hey, stop pushing me, patriot. I've got important news. Name's Chiminy Cricket—professional chiminy sweep."

I could see that Chiminy's long suit was soot. He had so much dirt it hurt.

Chiminy continued, "There's a traitor in town. Yessir, a real lowlife. Name's Benetick Arnold. He's gettin' ready to leak important information to the British. Something about an emergency ride to Lexington and Concord tonight, I think. He hangs out in there," Chiminy Cricket

said, pointing to a long orange and tur-
quoise building on the side of the road. "You
gotta find out what he knows."

Moving in for a closer look, I could see
that the building was, in fact, the first link
of a famous roadside restaurant and ice
cream parlor chain—Howard Johnsant's. I

figured the best way to check up on Benetick Arnold was to get a job as a waiter, so
I made a beeline for the manager's office.

I realized that finding out what Benetick
Arnold knew would take all the cunning I
could mustard. Good thing I'd taken the
time to catsup on my reading of American
history. I relished the opportunity to stop
Benetick before he could do any serious
damage to the patriots' cause—or to his own
neck. For I knew that given enough rope,
Benetick would hang himself.

Once inside the restaurant, my keen eye
quickly spotted Howard Johnsant himself.
Unfortunately, my other eye missed the
waiter coming toward me carrying a tray
piled high with hambuggers and French flies.

Pickling myself off the floor, I introduced myself to Mr. Johnsant. "What's the
scoop on this ice cream biz?" I asked
casually. "How many flavors have you got

so far?" In my time, Howard Johnsant's was famous for its 28 varieties.

"One," Mr. Johnsant answered. "But we're working on it."

"Revolutionary! Well, sounds as if you could use some new talent. And I'm just the bug to do it. Who do you think invented Rocky Roach? How about a job?"

Mr. Johnsant replied coldly, "You can certainly dish it out. But can you serve it?"

"Sher bet!" I responded cherrily, confident that I could fudge it.

Everyone was yelling for service. "Just a minute, men," I said calmly. Grabbing a tray, I headed for the nearest table.

Fortunately, my target was right in range. Benetick Arnold was furiously scribbling what I suspected to be the secret information onto a sheet of paper. I noticed that he wore the uniform of a patriot soldier—Colonel Grade Bee. I vowed silently to

myself, "Before this is over, I'll have your stripes, mister."

I sidled up to him and asked coyly, "How about some eggs, Benetick? Our specialty is Eggar Allan Poach. And by the way," I said slyly, hoping to trip up the offender, "haven't I seen you somewhere before? Another restaurant, perhaps? Traitor Tic's? Burger King George?"

"I doubt it," Benetick replied nervously. "You must have your signals crossed."

"No, no," I insisted. "You sound very familiar and I never forget a voice. You see, I have a phonographic memory."

At that point Howard Johnsant approached the table. "Phonographic memory, huh?" he said. "Sounds like a broken record to me. Is your brain scrambled?" he demanded. I could see this was no yoke. Obviously this waiter job was not all it was cracked up to be.

"Okay. No more Mr. Lice Fly," I muttered under my breath. "If you don't mind, I'd like to finish taking this order, Mr. Johnsant," I said icily. "Now," I said, removing the pencil from behind my antenna, "what'll it be?"

By this time that snake Arnold seemed quite rattled. Must have been my mention of Traitor Tic's. I'd just begun to viper his table when he recoiled and said shakily, "I'd like a Pesto Buzzmol. And a slice of good ole American apple pie."

I nearly choked as I ran toward the kitchen. The idea of that traitor hiding behind a patriotic pie! At least I didn't have to set the table. Benetick Arnold could eat his pie with his forked tongue. But when I returned with the order I was shocked to see that the fowl traitor had flown the coop. Ducked out on me. What a dumb cluck I'd been!

Then I saw it. Benetick Arnold's scribblings. Although he'd taken the paper he was writing on, the impressions made by his quill pen were still left in the placemat.

At first the strange writing appeared to have no rhyme or treason. I stared at the peculiar words for a minute before realizing that it was some sort of code. To anyone else, it might have looked like gibberish. But to me, it was as easy as pie. After all, gibberish is my middle name.

Here's what the placemat said:

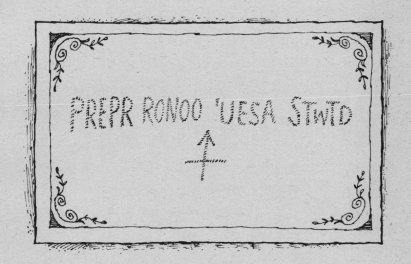

"Well," I said neatly to myself, "it's time to clean up another case. Not to mention the table. After all, I didn't get the Good Lousekeeping Seal for nothing!"

HOW DID INCOGNITO MOSQUITO BREAK
BENETICK ARNOLD'S CODE?

Incognito put two and two together. So what if he got three? Because our hero also realized that Benetick must have been using the old Evolutionary War Compass Code. Based on the four points of the compass—north, south, east, and west—it goes like this:

1. You write out your message normally.

2. You move around the compass clockwise, putting the first letter at north, the second at east, the third at south, etc.

3. Finally you write out the letters at each compass point, starting with north again. So when your message is written in code, you end up with four sets of letters—one for north, one for east, one for south, and one for west.

To break the code, you simply reverse the steps. The letters are numbered for you in Benetick's message to make it easier.

Put the four sets of letters back at the
points of the compass, starting with north:

```
        1   5  9  13 17
        P R E P R
              ↑
 4  8 12 16 20    N        2  6 10 14 18
S T W T D  ←W─┼─E→  R O N O O
              S
              ↓
        3  7  11 15 19
        ' U E S A
```

Write down the letters that are under the
numbers in order from 1 to 20:

```
1 2 3 4 5 6 7 8 9 10 11 12 13 14 15 16 17 18 19 20
P R ' S R O U T E N  E  W  P  O  S  T  R  O  A  D
```

Then break up the one big word into the
smaller words that make up the message:

PR'S ROUTE NEW POST ROAD

Incognito Mosquito understood Benetick's message because he knew his history.

He knew whose initials were PR. Paul Reverse! Our hero realized that Benetick Arnold was trying to tip off the British that Paul Reverse was taking the New Post Road.

Paul's important mission was to warn the colonests that the British were coming to attack their arsenal at Concord. It was the second part of his job, after signaling from the Old North Church how the British were leaving Boston: One if by land, two if by flea.

Once the colonests knew that Benetick Arnold had gotten word to the British of Paul Reverse's route, they simply "reversed" his route from the New Post Road to the Old Post Road. Why do you think he was called Paul Reverse anyway?

Benetick Arnold feared execution when he was tried for treason by a jury of his peers. Fortunately for him, it was a hung jury, so he wasn't. Yet.

As for Incognito, his reward was hearing Paul Reverse galloping down the road shouting "Two arms, four arms, six arms. The Yellow Jackets are coming! The Yellow Jackets are coming!"

After that "revolting" story, I realized I needed a breather. In fact, I could have used some artificial respiration. His attempts to repair the *Anterprise* had also left Mr. Mosquito somewhat breathless. He went to the pant-ry for something to drink but, finding it bare, suggested we go out for a bite. My mother told me never to have a bite with a mosquito, but then again, Mother had never met a mosquito like this.

As we left the apartment, the Mosquito flipped over a sign on the door—OUT TO LUNCH.

"That's for sure!" I thought.

On the way out I noticed Incognito's huge iron mailbox. "For chain letters," he explained.

Incognito Mosquito led me to a pleasant Chinese restaurant around the corner—Confusion's Inn. "Why don't we take the food back to the lab?" he suggested. "I always used to do takeout for a stakeout."

First we ordered egg rolls. The Mosquito commented on how crunchy they always were—"Must be the shell. But make them three-minute egg rolls. We're in a hurry. And why don't you give us some flied lice and an order of moo goo gai pun."

The Mosquito also ordered a side dish of lo mein because he said he needed to use his noodle. I guess I should have expected it. "Did you know that Marco Polo was the first to introduce spaghetti to the western world?" he asked. "It was actually

invented in China. Of course, that was
Marco's second important find. He also
discovered polo ponies, you know.

"Say, speaking of ponies, let me tell you
about my adventures in the Wild, Wild
Pest . . ."

3

The Case of the Missing Mustang

You would think that landing in a haystack would be ideal. And believe me it would have been—except for one thing. The pitchfork. I got the point. But I was fine except for a slightly deflated ego (among other things).

Much to my delight, I found myself in the middle of Buffalo Bill Cootie's Wild Wild Pest Show. Friends had been telling me for years to "go pest, young bug" and I mean, jumpin' fleahoshaphat! What red, white, and blue-blooded American bug wouldn't be excited about meeting the hero he read about as an elementary school pupa! This fella was a real big shot. My kinda guy. Why, he'd even ridden with the Punny Express!

Although I wasn't sure why I was here, I quickly assumed a disguise to make sure I fit in with the crowd. I was to be known as the Pundance Kid, fugitive from the I'm O.K./You're O.K. Corral Dude Ranch. The outfit even came with optional saddle sores.

This looked like the start of something big. I figured I might even pick up a few bucks at the rodeo by tackling a bull weevil or two. Then again, I recalled having tried my hand at cowpunching on a previous case.

All I got was a sore fist.

I was buzzy looking around at the sights when suddenly a scream pierced the air— not to mention my eardrum. In a flash I discovered its source—Wild Wild Pest star Annie Itchley, greatest sharpshooter of the frontier.

I rushed to the scene, arriving as Annie explained that she'd just seen somebody run off with her prize mustang. Unfortunately the barn was so dark that Annie hadn't seen much and the culprit got away.

"I just don't know what I'll do without my favorite horsefly. I may have to leave the show! Just thinkin' about the feller that stole him gives me an itchy chigger finger!" Annie said fiercely. "Why, I'd like to—"

I stepped forward and introduced myself to the petite Miss Itchley. "At your service, ma'am," I said, removing my hat and bowing so low that my gun belt landed around my neck. Fortunately, I didn't lose my head—or my gun—and calmly presented myself as the bug for the job.

"Listen here, Mosquito, you ole devil," she crowed. "You solve this case and catch the feller who stole my prize mustang, and my good old stallion Silverfish is yours. He's pure quarter horsefly," Annie said proudly.

"Gee, thanks, Miss Itchley," I replied graciously while examining Silverfish's teeth. "But what about the other three quarters?"

"You're not going to look a gift horsefly in the mouth, are you?" she asked.

"Annie, I'm surprised at you," I said disappointedly. "You may be quick on the chigger, but you should have known that you can't get a man with a pun."

I realized the best way to fit into a Wild Pest show was to be a wild pest. I found out quickly that I'd have no trouble getting hired by the show. The trick, in fact, was staying out of the show! Apparently many of Buffalo Bill Cootie's acts had been hired away by a rival Wild Pest show. But even that kind of setback couldn't keep a good bug down!

Or perhaps I should say clown. Because just at that moment a big red nose was slapped on my face and I was pushed into the arena in front of a cheering audience. I was terrified. In fact, I almost took off. But I suppose even the best of us gets stage flight. I calmed down and decided to do what comes naturally. I tripped over my own feet and generally made a fool of myself. The crowd loved it. They roared. So did the huge bull weevil behind me.

All of a sudden, there I was, precariously perched on the bull's horns. "Hey, where's the steering wheel on this thing?" I yelled. The bull tossed his head, and before I knew it I was flying over the grandstands. It was a great exit.

Annie Itchley's act was absolutely incredible. First a pagecoach appeared in the arena.

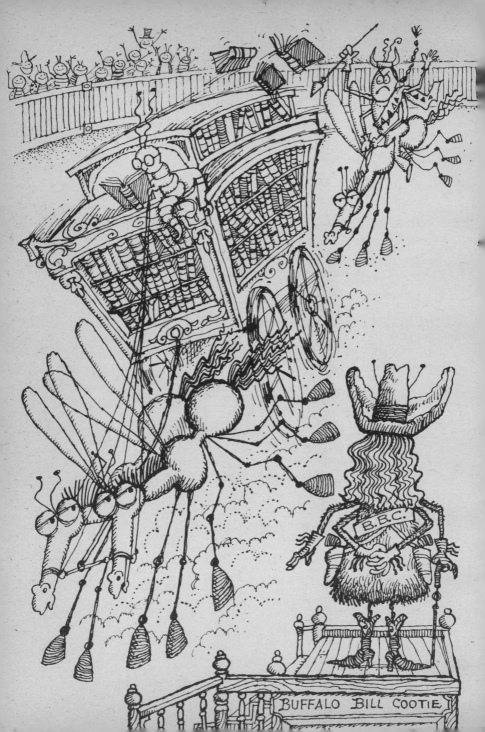

BUFFALO BILL COOTIE

The Wild Pest version of a library, these bookmobiles were essential in educating frontier bookworms. Then a tribe of wild Indians led by the famous Sitting Boll attacked the pagecoach. That was Annie Itchley's cue. She rode into the arena and singlehandedly fought off Sitting Boll and his group. Then came a demonstration of her shooting. Annie was such a sharpshooter that she could knock the head off a pin!

Next up was the famous French street singer Tic de la Rue, accompanied by Lee Noleum on the piano. Now don't think I'm an opra-tunist or anything, but I raised my hand to ask if Ms. La Rue took requests. She looked at me ruefully. I was dying to hear "Yellow Roach of Tixas." But she turned me down with a "duet yourself!"

So much for that lost cause. Next I ordered a piece of Custerd pie from one of the ringside stands, making sure to remind the fella behind the counter to "remember the à la mode!" Then I decided it was time for some serious insective work. I had to find out who stole Annie's horsefly.

I just couldn't understand why someone would want to steal her mustang. The culprit must have had some crazy reason. But what could his loco-motive be? I realized that this case was going to take some serious engine-uity. I was all steamed up and ready to go!

Immediately I was off to interview potential suspects. I tried everyone, starting with Buffalo Bill Cootie himself. He was a true showman, from the top of his pointy head to the tips of his long flowing boots. Make that from his long flowing hair to the tips of his pointy boots.

"Sorry, Mr. Mosquito," Buffalo Bill said sadly. "I'm afraid I don't have a clue as to who stole Annie Itchley's cowpony."

"Make up your mind, Buffalo Bill," I replied. "Which is it? A cow or a horse? You can't have it both ways."

Bill set me straight on the subject. I sure was a greenhorn about animals. "Just kiddin'," I said. "You know us rodeo clowns." I pointed to the big red nose that now matched the color of my face.

By sundown, I'd talked with most everyone in the show and the surrounding countryside, from Wild Bill Tickock to the town dentist, who in the Ole West was known as a gum stinger. Believe me, getting information out of that bug was like pulling teeth! But neither he nor anyone else for that matter knew anything about the theft of Annie Itchley's mustang.

My final stop was the tepee of Sitting

Boll. Even at this late hour, his camp-firefly was burning brightly. The big Indian seemed friendly enough, but when I asked him about Annie's horsefly, he simply raised his right hand and replied, "Ugh."

"Come now," I said. "Surely you can be more cooperative than that."

But all Sitting Boll would say was "Ugh."

I don't generally like to threaten suspects—especially when I thought I recognized some of the scalps hanging in his wigworm—but I said bravely, "Okay. Put up your dukes and fight like John Wayne. Anything you don't say may be used against you. What do you say to that?"

Sitting Boll calmly replied, "Sioux me."

By that time I was absolutely at my wits' end. Some say I didn't have far to go. "It's been a long day, Mosquito," Buffalo Bill said kindly. "Why don't you turn in?"

"Turn in to what?" I wondered sleepily as I made my way to my tent. But I found my path blocked by an old prospector and his mule, who Buffalo Bill said had been traveling with the show for a few days.

"This fellow's as stubborn as a mule," I

commented perceptively when the animal
refused to move.

"You show a keen grasp of th' obvious,
young feller," the old prospector agreed. "I
been prospectin' for near onto sixty years
now, and I ain't seen a more ornery animal
yet. Now that's one dad-blamed stubborn

mule. Darn shame too. Cause this mule's pappy was the best dang mule I ever did have."

Just then, it began to rain quite heavily. Us hearty western types are used to that. We just pulled up our collars and went about our business. All but the old prospector, that is. Before the first raindrop had hit the ground, he'd reached inside the mule's ample pack and pulled out a full-length raincoat. I already had my suspicions that this guy was not the old prospector he claimed to be. But pulling out a city slicker proved it.

The bug in question interrupted my thoughts by suggesting that he pull the front of the mule while I pushed from the back. Just at that moment, the mule decided to make his move. It was a rear-end collision, if you know what I mean—the mule's rear legs with my rear end.

Well, it didn't take a kick in the pants to tell me I was onto something here. I knew who had stolen Annie Itchley's mustang, and I had the culprit right where I wanted him. Unfortunately, the mule had me right where he wanted me. I was sorely tempted to make a citizen's arrest then and there. But I was even more sorely tempted to wait until I was out of range. Then I, too, closed in for the kick. . . .

WHY WAS INCOGNITO MOSQUITO SO SURE OF WHODUNIT?

Incognito was familiar with the birds and the bees. Not to mention the fleas in the trees. So he knew that mules are made by mating a horse with a donkey. Mules can't come from other mules because mules can't have children. (Although they can adopt.)

While lying about being a knowledgeable mule owner wasn't enough to convict the "prospector" of horsefly-napping, it was enough to arouse Incognito's suspicions. And anything that can arouse the Mosquito is worth checking out. After questioning, Incognito was finally able to get the bug to admit that he was indeed a city slicker, sent by a rival Wild Pest show to sabotage Buffalo Bill Cootie's operation. It seemed that the other show was losing customers due to Bill's popularity. By stealing Annie Itchley's prize horsefly, the bug planned to spoil Buffalo Bill's prize act and maybe even get Annie to quit the show.

Unfortunately the sneaky bug hadn't reckoned on reckoning with Incognito Mosquito. The Insective gave him several sharp cow pokes and sent him moo-ving along. The missing mustang was found in a nearby stable in stable condition.

His work done, Incognito jumped on the horse Annie had promised him. The stallion reared. Then he fronted as the Mosquito shouted, "Hi-yo, Silverfish!" and galloped away.

In the distance, a young boy was heard to ask, "Who was that bug?"

But of course that question was never answered. Our hero remained Incognito to the end.

"And so that's how the pest was pun," Incognito Mosquito concluded.

"As it turned out," he added proudly, "my insective work had an important effect on history. Had I not been able to recover Annie's horsefly, Buffalo Bill Cootie's show might have gone under. Ground, that is. Only the termites would have been able to catch it. And two very important spectators would have missed the spectacle.

"Thomas Aphid Edisant saw the show and went home with a great idea. The show inspired him to invent the electric lightning bug! Mark Twain was similarly

72

excited by Buffalo Bill Cootie's show. Although it had been said that 'east is east and pest is pest and never the Twain shall meet,' Mark was so impressed that he went home to write two famous books about the Mississippi River to prove that they could—*The Adventures of Hucklebuggy Finn* and *Lice on the Mississippi*!"

"Unbelievable," I said quite honestly.

The Mosquito was struggling with his *Anterprise*. It was hard to tell whether the strange noises I heard were coming from him or his machine. Once again, I asked the Mosquito if I could give him a hand. Any hand.

"I'm quite good with a wrench," I said wrenchingly.

But I could see that the Mosquito was getting impatient when he said crankily, "Give me that shaft."

"What a screwy nut this one is," I thought

to myself. "Say, what's in that box over there, Mr. Mosquito?" I asked, pointing to a small stone container. It was covered with fascinating markings.

"Oh, that," he replied. "That's a first aid kit from ancient Fleagypt. I won it three thousand years ago playing gin mummy."

When I opened the box I found all the usual first aid equipment—fliodine, Q-Tic swabs, and medicine for a variety of sicknesses common to that period, including cameline lotion for the humps and a special tonic for whooping sar-cough-agus.

"I really dig that ancient stuff," said the Mosquito. "That's why I decided to drop in on the Fleagyptians . . ."

4
The Unfair Pharoach Affair

My arrival in ancient Fleagypt was monumental. I landed in the hand of a huge stone statue. Needless to say, I was petrified. Looking down, I could see hundreds of Fleagyptians pointing up at

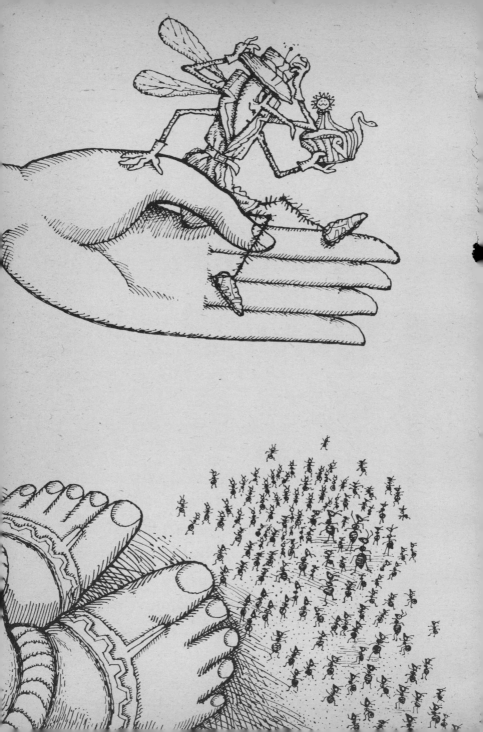

me with looks of wonder. From this height, they looked like ants. Then I realized they were ants. Still, I was pretty high up and afraid that I would slip through the statue's fingers. Fortunately at that moment I was under his thumb.

I did not remain idol for long. Discovering a hidden staircase, I slowly made my way down. "What a shame they haven't invented elevator shoes yet," I thought to myself.

Arriving at the ground floor, I found the Fleagyptians in an uproar. And I'd expected ancient Fleagypt to be quiet as a tomb! Everyone figured that I had to be some kind of god or something. They named me Mesquitaton, which roughly translated means "wooden-headed one who worships the sun," and carried me on their shoulders through the marketplace. There were bugs selling everything! When I asked "What's cookin'?" lettuce, bread, and raw eggs were immediately stuffed into my mouth. "Aha!" I chuckled to myself. "I've invented the Caesar salad and Julius hasn't even been born yet!"

It didn't take me long to find out what was going on in this place. I just checked out the flieroglyphics in the morning's news tablet, the *Herald Scribune*. Never let it be said that Incognito Mosquito can't read the handwriting on the wall!

An assassination attempt had just been made on the heir to the throne, the young Tutankhamant. Apparently he'd just es-

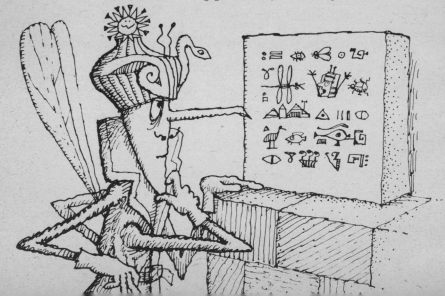

caped being stung by a carefully aimed poisoned dragonfly. Fingers—many fingers—were pointing at the crafty Pharoach, the current ruler. It seemed that the high priests had been trying to install young Tut as co-ruler against Pharoach's wishes.

One of the local merch-ants explained, "Pharoach has been mistreating everyone for years. He beats his mummies, leaves his beasts of burden in run-down camel lots, and even insists that the fish swim down the river one by one in a straight line—single Nile. He knows that young Tut will never permit this reign of terror to go on, so he tried to get rid of the ruler-to-be. But the Pharoach is also very tricky. No one can prove that he tried to kill Tut. And unless he's stopped, Pharoach will try again until he succeeds."

"Or until Tut secedes," I thought to myself.

I instructed the crowd to take me to the royal palace. Since I had been made an honorary god, I had no trouble getting in. The place fairly buzzed with activity. There were dozens of domesticks—mummy's helpers—herding hordes of royal children this way and that, playing ring-around-the-roachy and Simon stings. Royal scribes ran this way and that taking tictation. A select few were permitted to carve their messages into stone. This privileged group were known as the in-scribes.

I dropped in on young Tut just as he was finishing a pupaerus postcard to his mother-in-law, Nefertitic. It read, "Having a rotten crime. Wish you were heir!"

Although he was trying not to let the situation get to him, I could see that the poor kid was all wound up. He was so nervous that the minute I entered his throne room, I was throne out. "Tutchy, isn't he?" I thought to myself.

After I finally got back in to see Tut, it took several attempts before I could get him to say anything more than "No khamant." When I explained that I was a private insective, Tut eventually confirmed the people's story about the evil Pharoach. But while Tut, too, suspected the Pharoach of trying to kill him, he had no proof to make the accusation stick.

"No problem," I said breezily (which was more than I could say for the still desert

81

air—so torrid it was horrid). "Consider it done. Can you direct me to the Pharoach?"

"He is out in the Valley of the Kings supervising the construction of his tomb. You see," Tut explained, "we in Fleagypt believe in an afterlife. We spend eternity with our antcestors. So before we die, all rulers build themselves a beautiful tomb and stock it with all the things we will need after death for a peaceful voyage down the Nile. Of course, Pharoach went overboard. As you will see for yourself when you view his tomb. It is a long journey. You must go by camel."

And so I did. Arriving at the royal camel lot, I was asked by the keeper, "One hump or two?" Grinning, he handed a camel over to me. I asked cautiously, "Now, you're sure this is the best of burden?"

The ride turned out to be quite uncomfortable. If this camel was the best, I shudder to think about the worst. The camel was

fleabitten, and as a result was very wary
of insects. Also, she gave me a lot of lip—
though I came to understand that this was
not unusual for the breed.

Along the way I was distracted by many
amazing sights. There were hundreds of
bugs unloading tremendous stone slabs from
barges on the crickodile-infested Nile and
dragging them toward a half-finished pyr-
amid. I saw many bugs faint in the hot sun,
and watched as taskmasters whipped them.
My first impressions were confirmed—this
Pharoach was definitely *not* my kind of fly!

After a long and dusty ride, I finally arrived at the Valley of the Kings and introduced myself to the Pharoach inside his tomb. Boy! Talk about *Licestyles of the Rich and Famoth*! So this was how the other hive lives! The place was filled with furniture, sculptures, and sports equipment. Even the Pharoach's dishes shone with precious metal—gold-plated, I think. Speaking of shine, I could actually see myself in the polished stone of his sarcophagus. He obviously had a terrific burial chamber-maid!

The Pharoach himself was the most impressive of all. Decked out in gold and pre-

cious jewels, he glistened with every step. Not to mention clanked.

Surprisingly, the Pharoach was quite chariotable. He even invited me to dinner. He was serving lamb cheops. We ordered tomb service. Then he went so far as to offer a solution to the attempted assassination of Tutankhamant.

"You see," he explained, "I have a secret peephole in my private chamber that looks out into the great hall. Late one evening I

saw the head priestess tell one of her scribes to shoot a poisoned dragonfly at the ruler-to-be, our beloved Tutankhamant. So that's how I know who the culprit is."

I must have looked a bit puzzled at that point, because the Pharoach uttered a few cross words. I explained, "I was told that the priests and priestesses all favored Tut's co-ruling with you."

"Aha!" replied the crafty ruler. "The rumor is that they do. That's what they want the villagers to believe. But this high priestess realized that if Tut became co-ruler, one of the first things he would do is lower her salary and give the money to the people. And this she would not stand for. Although, of course, the head priestess would never admit it. We call her the queen of de-Nile, you know."

"Fortunate for Tut that you're watching out for him," I said. "But you know, you really shouldn't listen in on conversations. It's impolite to eavesdrop. Tut, tut.

"But thanks for the information," I said politely. "By the way, do you think I could see your private chamber?"

"Certainly," Pharoach replied. "I was just heading back to the city myself. Shall we go?"

You have no idea how relieved I was when Pharoach motioned for me to climb aboard a canopied litter. After my ride out to the Valley of the Kings, I swore I'd walk a mile not to ride a camel. The Fleagyptians might consider it "the ship of the desert," but just the thought of one made my heart sink.

The Pharoach clapped his hands suddenly, a dozen bugs picked up the litter, and we were off. Staring into his beady eyes, I realized that I didn't trust Pharoach. He was simply being too obliging about the whole thing.

It was nighttime when we finally arrived back at the palace. First the Pharoach showed me the great hall. It was lit up with hundreds of torches—a real hall of flame. The ruler pointed to the far end of the huge room. From where I was standing, I could see a decorated throne on top of a platform, surrounded by half a dozen huge stone columns.

"That, dear Mesquitaton," the Pharoach said, "is where I saw the high priestess plot against our Tut. Now, let me show you my private chamber."

We entered the Pharoach's private chamber next door to the great hall. It was some spread! He had servants whose only job was to peel grapes. And other servants who put the skins back on! He had dancing bugs as beautiful as Cleopaterpillar herself. And there were hundreds of soft pillows all over

the floor. I hadn't realized the Pharoach had such a cushy job.

Just as Pharoach had said, there was a peephole at one end of his chamber. And it did look into the great hall. But my keen insective sense told me something was wrong. "This case sphinks," I mumbled to myself as I put my eye to the hole. Somehow I didn't feel I was seeing the whole picture.

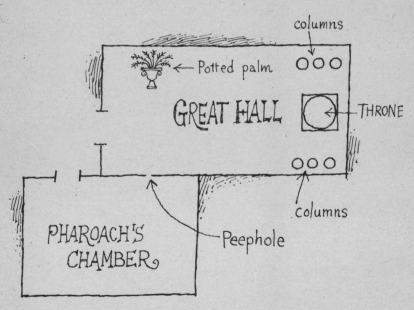

columns

← Potted palm

GREAT HALL

THRONE

columns

PHAROACH'S CHAMBER

Peephole

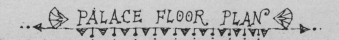

PALACE FLOOR PLAN

At that very moment I knew that my intuition was right. I hadn't paid for private insective school for nothing! I realized I'd wrapped up yet another case. Now for the loose ends.

"Pharoach," I said with a smile, "it's time to stop rocking the barge." His face turned to stone as I continued. "Admit it. You ordered the attempt on Tut's life and tried to frame the high priestess."

WHAT MADE INCOGNITO SUSPECT THE PHAROACH?

HERE'S WHAT:

The evil Pharoach actually trapped himself. Looking through the peephole at one side of the huge great hall, Pharoach couldn't possibly have seen the far end of the room—where he claimed to have seen the high priestess tell her servant to kill Tut. The view from a hole that small is very narrow.

WHAT INCOGNITO SAW

Tutankhamant went on to assume his rightful place on the throne of Fleagypt, under Incognito Mosquito's tut-elage, of course. He eventually built himself a magnificent tomb with enough loot in it it fill a museum.

The Pharoach got his just desert. Young Tut, tired of being plagued by his threats, dealt severely with the Pharoach, finally telling him, "Go to your tomb!" On the way out, the Pharoach gave Incognito the evil fly. The Mosquito just winked back.

"And that's why you should always take the broad view," concluded Incognito Mosquito.

"Ouch! I certainly got stung on that pun!" I thought to myself.

Apparently, the Mosquito was also stung, because he jumped back from the *Anterprise* quite suddenly. I guess he got quite a charge out of it. "Shocking," he muttered to himself. "I was positive that wire was negative!"

Once again I pleaded with him to let me help. "I really am quite good at fixing things, you know."

But to my annoyance, Mr. Mosquito still would not listen. He was quite single-minded. "Wouldn't it be a shame if this guy really did have a thought in his head," I thought to myself. "It would be like sentencing someone to solitary confinement."

The Mosquito looked closely at a dial and announced, "The *Anterprise* is almost empty. It's time to mix up a new batch of fuel. I try to do it only when absolutely necessary. You see, I have to sample each batch to make sure it's just right, and I've got to admit (chuckle, chuckle) the stuff gives me gas.

"Actually, I rely on my good taste quite a lot," the Mosquito said. "There was one time it even saved the day . . ."

5
The Merrie Olde Englant Mystery

I landed with a tree-mendous plop right in the middle of an old oak. Fortunately my fall was broken by a strategically placed fleahouse. Fortunately my back was not.

It took me a moment to get my bearings. My head was spinning in circles. At first I thought I'd landed on a king-sized bed. Suddenly I heard a groan. I realized I had landed on top of someone. "And a good moaning to you too," I said politely.

The squashee introduced himself as none other than the famed Friar Tick, a loyal member of Robin Hoodlum's Merry Band. I had landed back in the days (and knights) of yore (and mine)!

The good friar explained that the flea-house was a lookout tower to guard against surprise attacks by Robin's enemy, the evil marshal and tax collector—the Tariff of Gnattingham. Ever since good king Richard the Lion-heartwormed had gone off to fight in distant lands, his evil brother John had been using the Tariff to milk the peasants dry. They were all cowed by Prince John's rottenness and constant demands for moo-lah. Many were starving, unable to pay the ridiculous taxes that John demanded. The noble Sir Robin of Loxly gave up all his wealth and power to come to the aid of these poor bugs. He was robbin' from the rich and givin' to the poor, fighting John and his henchbug the Tariff at every turn.

Friar Tick and I went off to look for Robin deep in Sherwood Forest, munching on peanut cloisters and discussing what part I might play in the band—Friar Tick played the crumpet, but there were spots open for clarignat, fliolin, and ticcolo.

All of a sudden we were jumped by a group of thugs and I was blindfolded, tied up, and roughly led away. I struggled, but my efforts were feudal. I suppose the roughnecks would have taken the friar, too, if they'd had the bugpower. But I guess they weighed the alternatives and decided to scale down the undertaking after seeing the gravity of the situation.

As I was hustled along it became clear that my kidnappers had mistaken me for one of Robin Hoodlum's Merry Bugs. They had been sent by the Tariff of Gnattingham to nab one of the band. Why? I didn't know. But I was bound and determined to find out.

The road to the Tariff's hiveaway was long and winding. "Gee," I thought to myself, "nightfall fell pretty fast around here. It sure got dark in a hurry." Then I remembered the blindfold. I also remem-

bered how hungry I was. After all, I'd had barely a bite in over eight hundred years! And right at that moment I could smell the delightful aroma of fresh bread.

"How about a little lunch?" I asked my captors ryely, trying to worm a small mealy out of them. "I'd be glad to pay for it. I've got plenty of dough. I'd even give you a dime for a pumpernickel. A loaf of whole wheat? Half wheat?"

But of course the Tariff's men wouldn't listen. Their money was measured in pounds, and my offer of dimes didn't carry any weight with them.

Besides, my pleas were soon drowned out by the sounds of a crowd of children laughing and shouting. My head was swimming. And my captors wouldn't throw me a lifesaver. Or even an M & M! Then a bell rang. The children started running. Then there was silence.

"Strange place, this medweevil time zone," I thought to myself. "Sure wish I could get away. If I could just get my hands on a weapon." I hummed softly to myself, "If I had an armor. . . ."

Just then I felt heat on my face. "Is this the end of the line?" I wondered. "Neigh, it never happens like this in the movies," I assured myself as we forged ahead. I took a few deep breaths and was just cooling off when all of a sudden there was a taste of salt in my mouth. "How about some pepper?" I chived my kidnappers. But my wit was wasted on my seasoned opponents, I realized as I continued gingerly, keeping thyme with my kidnappers.

Soon afterward we arrived at the Tariff's secret hiding place, miles from the forest prime-weevil. It was there that my blindfold was at last removed, and I met the evil bug himself, who explained his plan to me.

"I've wanted Sir Robin of Loxly—this Robin Hoodlum—for a long time. Now I've finally figured out how to get him," the Tariff sneered. "And once I get him, it will mean the downfall of King Richard the Lion-heartwormed. His brother John will take over the rule of England and I will be his right hand. Or at least one of them.

"I'm going to use you as bait," the Tariff went on. "I'll send Robin a message that he can have you back only if he gives himself up. Robin is such a Goodfellow that he'll certainly trade his own life for yours. When he shows up at the spot I've picked, you will be released and I'll bring Robin here. Since you were brought to my hiveaway blind-folded, there's no way you can show Robin's band where it is."

"Tariff, you are an evil bug," I said accusingly. "I knew you and Robin Hoodlum were archer enemies, but I never thought

you'd bow this low! Robin may not always
follow the straight and arrow, but I know
that his relentless fight for good will win
out."

The Tariff of Gnattingham turned out
to be right on target about Robin's loyalty.
At the appointed hour Robin showed up at
the spot that the Tariff had selected for the

exchange and I was returned to the Merry
Band. Who naturally were not so merry
anymore.

William Scarlett had turned a bright
crimson, and the lovely Maid Mariant was
crying softly. For her and Robin it had been
love at first flight. Little John was muttering
something about having to scour the forest

or scrub the entire band on account of Robin's kidnapping. Worst of all, Friar Tick was about to step on me.

"If it wasn't for you, Robin wouldn't be in this mess!" the friar said. "You make me burning mad. But you're no match for me. I'm wholly of a mind to stamp you out!"

MacFlea, a Scotch tapeworm in the band,

suddenly grabbed me with his sticky hands and shook me. "Let me go!" I yelled. He loosened his grip. Good thing too. He nearly brogue my arms. I hoped he felt kilty about it.

"Hey, wait a minute!" I cried. "I've heard of being downtrodden, but this is ridiculous. Besides, I always planned to die a gnatural death—acute hardening of the archeries or something. And whatever happened to all for pun and pun for all?"

I think that last remark must have worked. So I marked it again. "There's nothing to worry about. I can tell you exactly where to find Robin. Even though I'was blindfolded on the way to the Tariff's hideaway, I still had five other senses to rely on—hearing, smell, taste, touch, and . . . my unfailing sixth sense—nonsense.

"Now just bring me a map and I'll get to the route of this kidnapping caper." The band found a map of the area and spread it out on the table in front of us. "Ah, here we go. Let me show you the route we took."

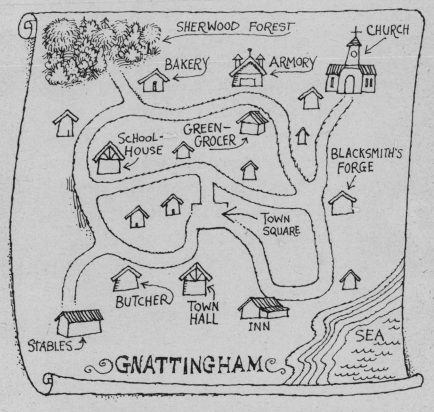

HOW DID INCOGNITO MOSQUITO KNOW THE ROUTE TO THE TARIFF'S SECRET HIVEOUT?

It was simple work for our hero to retrace his steps to the Tariff of Gnattingham's secret hiveout. Incognito realized that the fresh bread he smelled must have come from a bakery. The noises he heard were children playing in a schoolyard—when the bell rang, recess was over and they all ran back to their classroom. That accounted for the sound of running and then quiet. Then Incognito felt heat because he passed a blacksmith's forge. Finally, the taste of salt in his mouth came from the sea.

By connecting all of these points, Incognito and Robin Hoodlum's Merry Band were able to pinpoint the location of the evil Tariff's secret hideaway.

All that remained was for Robin's band to sneak through the trees and am-bush the captors. The plot was successful and Sir Robin was quickly restored to Sherwood

Forest. Maid Mariant, who was known all over the medweevil countryside as "the hostess with the moatstess," threw Incognito a huge banquet.

Then Robin Hoodlum himself did something totally unnecessary and unexpected which proved him to be the cream of the cheese.

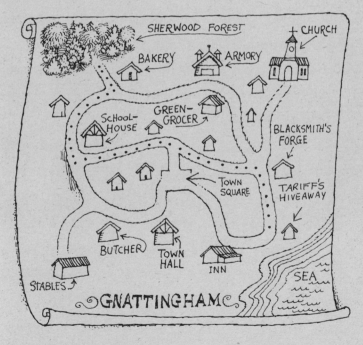

• • • • • ROUTE OF KIDNAPPING

To show his gratitude, Sir Robin be-
stowed upon Incognito the unofficial title
of Sir Mosquito of Bagels. Then his Merry
Band played "Flea for Two" as the pair—
the Knights of Bagels and Loxly—walked
arm in arm in arm in arm into the sunset.

It took me a moment to get hold of myself. The thought of a goofball like Incognito Mosquito tinkering with history was more than I could bear. I mean, here was a bug who was absentminded twenty-five hours a day! Why, he couldn't even fix his own time machine. Much less time itself!

I wondered just how far the Mosquito would go. I wasn't about to follow him to the ends of the earth or anything, but this gimmick was just too good to drop just yet. "Tell me, Mr. Mosquito," I asked. "Did you take other trips back into history? I mean, besides the ones you've told me about?"

"Naturally," the Mosquito replied. "Why, I knew Plymoth Rock when it was just a pebble. And I met Peter Flyvesant when he was the governor of New Antsterdam.

young Plymouth Rock

Governor Flyvesant of New Antsterdam

He had a wooden leg, you know. But he was quite limber on his timber.

"Do you realize that I watched William Shakespeare struggling with his most famous play? He came up with the idea over

Breakfast with the Bard

breakfast. That's why he made the hero a Danish. He was going to call the play *Ham Omelette*. But I said to him, 'Bill, Bill! You've got to make it short and catchy for the public's taste. You're muffin' it! *Ham Omelette* is no good. You've gotta leave 'em bacon for more.'

"'Aha!' said Bill. 'I think I see what you're driving at. How about something like *Hamlet*?'

"'Totally up to you, Bill, to decide whether it's to bee or gnat to bee.'

"'Can I quote you on that, Incognito?' Bill asked. 'Say, tell me, have you ever considered playwriting?'

"'Thanks, but no thanks, Bill,' I replied modestly. 'It's just not in my blood. After all, you've got to know flyself.'"

Ouch! This mosquito was too much. He was the real tragedy if you ask me. And there was no turning the bug off.

"And who do you think was there to lend Teddy Roachevelt his American Distress Card when Teddy yelled 'Charge!' and then remembered he'd forgotten his plate? I never leave hive without it. And I'd be able to go on solving crimes throughout history if I could only fix this time machine of mine! But I guess you can't teach an old bug new tics."

"But Mr. Mosquito!" I cried. "That's what I've been trying to tell you all this time! I can fix your machine!"

"I'll fix his machine all right," I thought to myself. "Who cares if I never sell him a magazine subscription? Does he think I believed all of those crazy stories about time travel? I know as well as he does that this 'time machine' is just a pile of scrap iron. And he thought he'd test my metal. Hah! Now, just a few more turns on that screw, a tap here with the hammer . . . and

I'll make this hunk of junk puff smoke in the ole mosquito's face."

"There, Mr. Mosquito," I said. "It's good as new. Want to take her out for a spin?" I asked.

"Well, okay," the Mosquito said doubtfully as he climbed into the *Anterprise*. But when he switched on the ignition, a strange thing happened. Instead of the machine backfiring, the dials on the dashboard began to spin wildly. The date adjustment numbers were getting higher and higher! It looked like I was sending Incognito Mosquito, Private Insective, into the future!

Just then the Insective yelled, "Bug Rogers of the twenty-first century, look out!"

And in a puff of smoke, he was gone. Who knows what time zone he'll show up in next. Maybe . . . even yours!

About the Author

E. A. Hass shares a New York City apartment with two lazy, literate cats. In the summer there are usually several dozen mosquitoes around as well, any one of which could be *the* mosquito.

E. A. buzzes around doing all kinds of things, many of which involve two favorite subjects—children and books. In addition to being an author and publicist, Hass appears as Dr. Book on American Public Radio's *Kids America* show, diagnosing book ailments and dispensing prescriptions for good reading. Example: "Candy is dandy but books won't rot your teeth!"

About the Artist

Don Madden lives with his wife, son, and daughter in an old farmhouse in upstate New York. They share the place with a large scraggly dog and a small flabby cat, who spend their time trading fleas. Before moving to the country Mr. Madden studied and taught at the Philadelphia Museum College of Art. Now he illustrates children's books and fights off hordes of six-legged visitors.